To

You Know You're Getting Older When...

by Lois L. Kaufman and Evelyn Beilenson

Illustrated by Lyn Peal Rice

PETER PAUPER PRESS, INC.
WHITE PLAINS, NEW YORK

For us

Copyright © 1994
Peter Pauper Press, Inc.
202 Mamaroneck Avenue
White Plains, NY 10601
All rights reserved
ISBN 0-88088-614-5
Printed in China

7 6 5 4 3

Introduction

Whether we're 30, 40, or 50, we know we're getting older. We like to think it's all in our minds, but sometimes our bodies remind us that if we're pushing 40, that's exercise enough.

As the years pass, our old passport pictures seem to reflect a better image than we remembered, and our rosy cheeks may come from hot flashes.

We're not as young as we used to be, but we're not as old as we're going to be, either! So let's continue to look at aging with a sense of humor. Remember that wrinkles are where the smiles have been, and, like fine wine, we improve with age.

—L.L.K. and E.B.

You Know You're Getting Older When...

Driving a man wild
is done by
hiding the remote control.

GERRRRRR

You Know You're Getting Older When...

Making out means
reading the small type on the menu.

You Know You're Getting Older When...

Skinny dip means something low calorie
to eat with raw vegetables.

You Know You're Getting Older When...

Happy hour is the period of time
when nothing hurts.

You Know You're Getting Older When...

Shopping counts as exercise.

You Know You're Getting Older When...

An antique is something your mother
bought new.

You Know You're Getting Older When...

It's ten o'clock and you don't *care* where your children are.

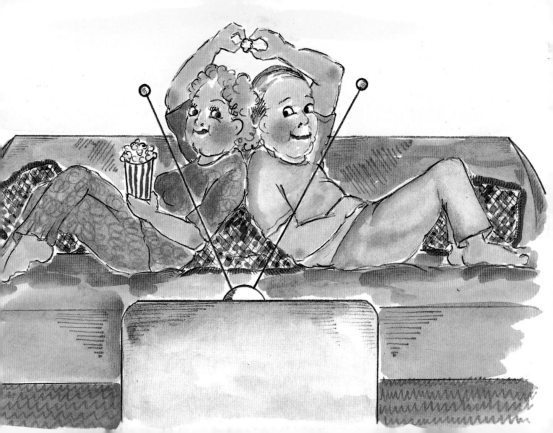

You Know You're Getting Older When...

A walk on the wild side means
taking your dog out.

You Know You're Getting Older When...

You wish you had worn ear plugs instead of earrings to the wedding reception.

You Know You're Getting Older When...

You remember sex as dirty and the air as clean.

You Know You're Getting Older When...

The early movie starts after your bedtime.

YOU KNOW YOU'RE GETTING OLDER WHEN...

A hot flash is not the latest news report.

You Know You're Getting Older When...

"Some settling may occur" refers to you,
not the cereal.

You Know You're Getting Older When...

The best man for the job
turns out to be a woman.

You Know You're Getting Older When...

You feel like getting on line behind your car at the body shop.

You Know You're Getting Older When...

What's behind you
is larger than
what's ahead of you.

You Know You're Getting Older When...

"Sir" or "Madam" doesn't sound like
a term of respect.

You Know You're Getting Older When...

Getting a lift no longer means
getting a ride home.

You Know You're Getting Older When...

Lifetime membership doesn't seem like such a bargain.

You Know You're Getting Older When...

Your legs buckle but your belt doesn't.

You Know You're Getting Older When...

A false alarm doesn't mean you mistakenly thought you were pregnant.

You Know You're Getting Older When...

Having it all means remembering today
what happened yesterday.

You Know You're Getting Older When...

Your age and your height in inches are
the same number.

You Know You're Getting Older When...

You've forgotten the "affair to remember."

You Know You're Getting Older When...

Santa Claus begins to have real sex appeal.

You Know You're Getting Older When...

You keep trying to lose weight but it keeps
finding you.

You Know You're Getting Older When...

Your insurance costs more than your car.

You Know You're Getting Older When...

Sex becomes a job, and you've joined the ranks
of the unemployed.

You Know You're Getting Older When...

Your birthday cake candles set off the smoke alarm two rooms away.

You Know You're Getting Older When...

You are likely to expire before
your driver's license does.

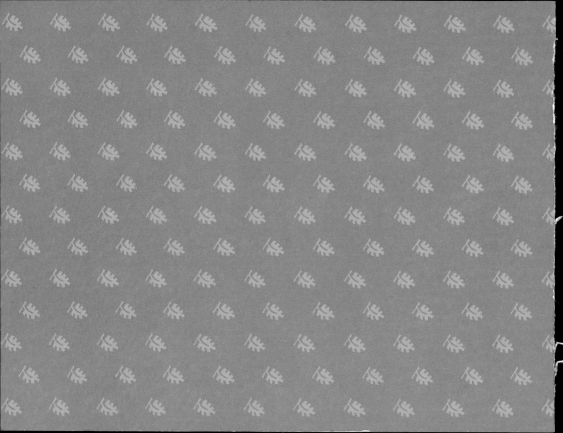